I See Things
In Blue

I See Things In Blue
I

Dario

Samuel Alexander

Table of Contents

Anxious

Dario was anxious as he stood off-stage waiting to perform. He had just finished his piano solo for the recital but still had a song to sing. The thought of the crowd watching him, the fitting of the mic to his height and the guitarist getting ready to play was too much for him. Hiding off stage seemed the most logical solution. Now, however, he was nervous about the wait to be called back on stage. Anxiety attack not averted.

Dario got anxious when things didn't go smoothly. He probably should've stayed on stage since standing off stage was yielding the same results. Although only five years of age, the signs of anxiety issues were very prevalent. As he stood, waiting in the shadows, it seemed as if the moment dragged on forever. He could hear his mother in his head, blaming his anxiety on weakness. "Nothing prayer and God couldn't fix," she would say.

After what felt like an eternity of waiting, Dario was signalled back onstage. He did as instructed and walked towards the mic, trembling; a nervous hot-mess hearing the sound of encouragement from the crowd. Instead of helping this made him think more of his impending failure.

Barely aware of his own self on stage, Dario tried to block them out. The bright lights shining on his face giving him something to focus on other than the audience. It didn't work. When the cue came for him to sing, nothing happened.

This was his first public solo, but If he didn't sing it might not be. The guitarist kept extending the intro because Dario couldn't get a note out. The audience fell into deathly silence as the suspense of whether he would sing, walk off stage, or start crying filled the hall. The atmosphere tensed with only the sound of the guitar filling the void.

There came a point when the guitarist started to hum. The tone that escaped him was smooth and calming. It caught Dario by surprise, influencing him to turn and look. The guitarist had his eyes closed. Lost in what looked like a magical space to Dario as he watched fingers dance to improvised sounds waiting for him to find the courage to sing. Eventually, the musician opened his eyes to see a mesmerised Dario watching him and smiled. Dario smiled back, somehow found the voice he was missing, turned towards the audience and sang.

Food Siblings and Tears

At age seven, Dario's anxiety had become more intense. His parents contributed to this by often telling him it was some flaw of character only prayer could fix. Dario was very self-sufficient for his age. He woke up and got ready for school without prompting. Even ironed his clothes on a child-sized ironing board his mother found for him.

A lot of this independence came from a desire for approval. Dario thought it would make his parents, especially his mom, happy. She didn't disapprove. That was more than enough for Dario.

Today was more of the same. Dario got ready, then went to the kitchen prepared for breakfast in perfect school attire. Not a hair out of place. He sometimes thought he saw a smile creep into the corner of his mother's eyes mornings. He wasn't sure, though.

Dario's breakfast was perfectly proportioned. He'd gotten into watching nutrition stations on TV and insisted on eating healthy. His mother obliged pretending like it wasn't her fault this obsession had arrived. A few weeks previously, she saw him eating junk food and said,

"If you keep eating like this, you'll turn into a disgusting blob that no one could love."

It was odd because as his parent she was the one providing the food. It was as if she purchased it on purpose so she could berate him. This truth was lost on Dario. He didn't eat dinner that day. Instead, he went to his room and cried.

Moments into his crying his mom came in holding his brother, claiming Dario's barely audible sobs were the reason he was also crying.

"You can both cry together," she said, then left the room. Dario helped his brother up into the bed. His brother, Drake, was coming up on his second birthday.

Dario didn't know why, but he couldn't cry with Drake. He took him into his arms and sung to him. Singing was the answer to everything. He crooned his brother to sleep and fell asleep shortly after.

The next day, still in the emotions from the previous night, Dario only ate a small lunch at school. This lead to one day where he didn't eat at all and teachers started asking questions he couldn't answer.

Dario decided there had to be foods that wouldn't make him gross and started looking up things online. Within days he was shopping with his parents for healthier foods and had convinced his dad to do morning runs with him. Now, weeks later, he was eating a perfectly balanced meal in an immaculately pressed outfit after another morning run that his dad was not excited about. Exercise was overrated as far as his father was concerned.

"How do you feel about kickboxing," his father asked.

Dario said okay and ate an apple slice. He was already playing football. What's one more activity? His dad liked football, and his mom never missed a chance to talk about how good of an athlete their son was. Like he was going to be the next NFL superstar at age seven. Always with the praise in public spaces but never in private.

After breakfast, Dario followed his mother outside as she was going to be driving him to school. Upon arrival, before letting him out of the car, she said,

"You had better not get into any trouble today."

Dario assured her he would be nothing but the most well-behaved boy he could be. His mom, unfortunately, didn't seem moved by his assertations and hurried him out of the car.

Dario was looking forward to meeting up with his two friends today, Gavin and Rayland. It was the highlight of every school day for him. They were so close there was a picture of the three of them naked in a tub amongst the many photos Gavin's mom could not stop taking of them. He greeted them as they entered the classroom shortly after he did. The three of them talked for a while. Rayland and Gavin did most of the talking, Dario speaking only when necessary. The three of them quieted down once class began.

***

Dario was alone listening to music and reading a book during lunch break when someone called him blue; loud enough to hear through his headset. They followed that up by telling him his eyes matched his shirt. Then other children started taunting him. Dario was the shade of deep, rich honey. Not the lighter golden kind people immediately associate honey with. He tried to not look people in the eye too much because he thought he was too dark for blue eyes. It made him very uncomfortable, and the other kids knew it.

Today Dario's instinctive reaction was to punch the first kid in the face, and before he knew it, Rayland and Gavin were there helping him and lunch turned into a fight that no one was safe from. Since so many kids were involved, it was hard to determine who was at fault and putting the entire class behind for detention was not something the teacher seemed willing to do. This lead to everyone but no one getting in trouble for this fight.

Dario couldn't understand why the other students wouldn't leave him alone. He had previously begged his parents to let him wear coloured contacts, but they said he was too young. To make things worse, his glasses got broken in the fight, and these were his backup pair. The last were lost in another fight a few days before when. Calling him a freak. He hit her. She punched him knocking off Dario's glasses then stepped on them for good measure.

The rest of the day went by uneventful. Dario was glad for this because his anxiety was making it hard to concentrate. All he did was try to be the perfect child then fights happened. His friends attempted to make him feel better, but Dario just remained on edge the rest of school, thinking about the car ride home. When he'd have to explain the missing glasses.

***

Dario stood with the rest of the kids waiting for their parents to drive up to the entrance and retrieve them. Rayland and Gavin waved bye to him as their rides came before his. Both laughing and unbothered by the lunchtime fight. Already arguing with their parents about how they were right and everyone else was wrong before even getting into their separate cars and leaving.

Dario didn't understand this. He tried never to argue about anything with his parents, and these two argued all the time with theirs and seemed so much happier than him. What was he doing wrong?

When his mother's car came up in the cue. Dario walked down to get in; sitting in silence as he always did the entire drive home. When they walked into the house, she said,

"Go to your room, do your homework, and don't come out until you're done."

Dario liked school. He hated when his mother made him not want to do his work because it felt like she was taking something away from him. She always did that. Refused to let him enjoy anything unless on her terms and his dad never discouraged her. The only thing she couldn't take though was singing. That was his and his alone. He walked into his room put on his headset, picked his classical music playlist and got to work; hoping he could reclaim the joy that was schoolwork back despite his mom's best efforts to ruin it.

At dinner, there was more silence. Dario was hoping nothing would be said. That she wouldn't mention the broken glasses but,

"…weak if you can't take a few taunts. You're nothing but trouble, and that is the second pair of glasses you have ruined this month."

Dario didn't know what to do except apologise. His mother scoffed. His dad agreed because he was the one buying the new glasses. Dario lowered his head in shame. He got up to put his dishes in the dishwasher and could feel her looking at him and instinctively looked up. His mother practically growled at him before saying,

I See Things In Blue: Dario

"You don't deserve those eyes."

Dario held in his tears until he got to his room. Somewhere in the corners of his mind, he believed her. She said it often enough, and all the children teased him about it. His dad never stood up for him, so obviously what she said was true. The only two who didn't care were Rayland and Gavin. Dario believed that maybe if he were a better son, all this negative energy would go away. It hadn't yet, but he was hopeful.

While pondering his family situation, Drake entered the room. Dario helped him up onto the bed and found the will to stop the tears. He silently vowed that he would be the type of boy any parent would love and want. No matter what that took. If they desired perfect, he would be more than.

Church, Friendship and Ties Undone

Two years had passed and reaching age nine brought no new insights on how to make his parents happy. It was a youth Sunday at church. Dario, Rayland and Gavin were sitting together with other children as part of the church youth choir. The choir was positioned in the first three centre rows in front of the altar. Dario and his friends were positioned on the left aisle side in the first row. Not Dario's favourite position as he'd rather hide amongst the other children.

Dario's mother was the chosen speaker this Sunday. This meant he would be quizzed about her sermon during the car ride home or over Sunday brunch should they head out to eat. Dario didn't realise it, but this was her way of finding something to be mad at him about. A useless enterprise because Dario would never forget to pay attention.

Gavin and Rayland, however, were the complete opposite. Always chatting about something or other in church. Small talk wasn't Dario's strong point, so he let them talk around him. As he was sat between them he didn't really have a choice but to let them talk around him. He was fully capable of focusing on church while pretending to be part of their chatter at the same time.

At some point during service, probably out of boredom, Gavin pulled at Dario's shirt, which Dario quickly straightened. Rayland, following Gavin's lead, messed up Dario's tie. Straightening the tie in his seat was not an option. Dario had to leave and retie it properly with a mirror.

Shortly after re-joining his friends, Rayland and Gavin moved to mess Dario's clothes again. The look Dario gave them halted their actions. It did nothing, however, to stop them from laughing. *Why can't they just be decent well-behaved children and pay attention,* Dario tried to ponder the thought but Gavin started talking to him.

"You need to lighten up Dario."

Gavin ate a packaged chocolate chip cookie than offered Rayland one.

"You're not supposed to be eating in church."

The mortified look on Dario's face was priceless. Gavin decided not to push it and put the rest of the cookies away. Rayland ate hers and Dario gave her a sigh of disapproval.

"What? Gavin can't be the only one enjoying cookie goodness."

Dario continued to glare at her and Rayland simply shrugged and demanded Gavin give her another cookie. He didn't put up much resistance and also ignored the look Dario gave him.

"Look I'm just here to sing. Not to play by the rules. I'm going to be a superstar."

Dario saw this conversation as a lost cause and decided to get his mind back in the service. It wasn't long before Rayland and Gavin ended up arguing prompting an adult to shush them and making Dario wish he wasn't sitting with them.

"I'm trying to listen. Could you two please stop distracting me? And nothing when my mom is finally up."

Dario knew if he got frustrated enough, they would leave him alone; pretend to be as interested in church he was. He didn't care if they were faking it only that they did it.

"Finally. They are calling us up to sing. Seriously there is no other reason to be here."

Gavin nodded in agreement, but Dario refused to acknowledge Rayland's comment. He would never admit his sole purpose for being interested in church was because of his parents. If they believed Christianity was important, then it was important to him. The real truth was he felt exactly as Rayland did. Singing was the only reason to be there, but he was not ready to admit that even if only by agreement.

After church, the three of them walked to a quiet spot to help Dario escape the crowds. Rayland and Gavin didn't care much, but if Dario wanted to break away, they would break away with him.

"Man, you are so neat. How do you always look so clean?" Gavin said. Dario couldn't tell if Gavin was impressed, amused or confused.

"He knows how to use an iron, Gavin. A skill you could definitely use."

"I'm nine. My mom irons all my clothes."

"So is he. What's your point?"

"There is no point really," Gavin said, slightly shrugging his shoulders. "So, you guys coming by my place this weekend?"

"Sure. I could use a day without my parents talking about all this money I'm going to be making for them. Like I'm going to share my future millions with them. Besides, your brother is cute."

"Eww. I didn't need to know that. And he's almost eighteen. He's too old for you."

Rayland looked at Gavin as if to say age could never get in the way of her dreams. Dario laughed as the two of them chatted. He was definitely looking forward to spending time with them. Gavin's parents did not go to church. Dario didn't understand this because church was life.

Gavin was so different from himself, Dario thought as he looked at his friend. Not as clean. Not as good in school. He was forever failing, then passing, then failing. Dario had no idea if he was smart and lazy, stupid and lucky, or some weird combination of both.

Rayland was as extroverted as it got. The girl had no fear as far as Dario could tell. She was taking voice lessons, most forms of dance, and acting classes. She had even gotten Dario into dance classes by brute force. He didn't really have a choice. Dario often pointed this out to her when she tried to make it seem as if he decided dance would be good for him.

"So are you coming or not. Or are you just going to be boring and stay home and read a book," Rayland said with an epic eye-roll. It was time for Dario to get out his own head and join the conversation. Maybe they wouldn't expect too much from him.

"I like reading."

Rayland chuckled, "You know I'm only playing. His mom makes a good lasagna, and you can't eat so healthy all the time."

Dario sighed. He could go for some lasagna. He had already made up his mind and was only waiting for them to prompt him to verbalise it. At least that was how it played out in his mind. In truth, the two were stalling until it seemed like he was willing to talk.

"Yeah, I'll come by."

Lasagna and Self-Revelations

Dario preferred when his Dad drove him places. The week had ended and he was now just pulling up outside of Gavin's house. Dario's mother refused to take him for some reason. As far as he knew, Gavin's parents were always nice to her so Dario couldn't figure out why she avoided them outside of school if she could. He tried to ask his father on more than one occasion, but every time he did his father's mood would change, so Dario stopped asking.

"Enjoy some real food Dario.".

Dario smiled, and his dad leaned in and kissed him on the forehead. Fleeting and rare as this extra bit of something was, it was enough for Dario to like him just a bit more than his mom.

"But you and mother said—"

"Your body is the temple of the Lord. I know. But I'm sure even Jesus ate a bag of chips sometimes."

Dario didn't respond, just nodded. He had his prepacked healthy meals and would probably only add a smidge of lasagna just to shut up his friends. At the moment he was taking extra time getting out of the car. Sitting in silence. Mildly annoyed that even for a visit to his friends, he still anxious.

Eventually Rayland and Gavin came out and ushered him into the house. Grabbing Dario's things for him acting completely natural about his situation.

***

"Dario. Look at you all cute as ever." Gavin's mom was forever telling Dario he was cute, and over-hugging him. The only person other than his friends and family, including Louis', he was okay with being touched by.

"Enough, mom! Let the boy breathe. Honestly. You don't love me that much. I'm your son."

"Don't remind me. Satan's spawn."

Both Gavin and his mother began a staredown. These standoffs, while entertaining, could drag on forever. Gavin caved first this time.

"Fine. I don't need your hugs anyway!"

Gavin's mom pulled her son into a ridiculously exaggerated hug. Gavin protested and tried his hardest to escape, but to no avail.

"Alright. I love you too, ma."

She smiled in satisfaction, then kissed him. Gavin's guard came down, and he smiled back. Rayland rolled her eyes. She was used to their fake non-love rituals, amusing as they were. Dario thought if he shouted at either of his parents, he'd be dead. Then he realised he would never yell at them so that scenario was unlikely to present itself.

"I cleared out a whole shelf for you for the weekend. I even made a nice small whole wheat lasagne for you and you alone."

"Yuck. Pasta should not be good for you."

Rayland made a disgusted face as she helped Gavin's mom load up the shelf. Dario was happy they didn't find his obsession with prepared healthy meals weird. The kids at school teased him all the time. It didn't help that he wore glasses and loved to read. He sometimes wished he was cooler. Being teased did nothing for his anger and anxiety issues.

Dario thanked them for helping him, then went to Gavin's room. It was exceptionally clean. Dario knew Gavin and Rayland tried to one-up each other on cleanliness when he went to their houses. He pretended not to notice their bit of rivalry though.

"I made a space for you over there," Gavin said as he pointed over to a corner that was immaculately cleaned. Not just stuff moved aside. Gavin had made a space for Dario to Dario's standards. Rayland was already in the bed refusing to acknowledge the smug look on Gavin's face. Dario neatly arranged his clothes then forced Rayland and Gavin to get their school work done.

I See Things In Blue: Dario

Gavin's room was bigger than his, as was his bed. Dario was shorter than both of them, so the need for a big bed wasn't necessary. Still, he couldn't deny the perks of a large bed.

Dario put on his pyjamas; pausing for a second after he turned, looking towards the bed. Upon coming out of a brief trance, Dario was unsure how long he had spaced-out, or if anyone had noticed.

"I *hope no one saw that,"* was his only thought as he began to walk. Dario pulled out his Bible to read a few verses before settling in.

"You're not going to wake us up tomorrow when you go for your run?"   Rayland was not a fan of having her sleep interrupted when it didn't have to be. Especially on a Saturday morning. Thankfully Gavin's mom was a Sunday cleaner and not a Saturday morning cleaner so she wouldn't have to endure being forcibly awoken like back home.

"You could just come with me."

Rayland scoffed and made sure he knew he had to sleep on the edge of the bed closest to his clothes. She was not doing anybody's run.

"Louis said he'd run with me."

"So is this going to become a real thing? Dad finally giving up?"

Gavin laughed. He knew his own mother would run with Dario but still found it amusing Dario's dad was ready to give up. And even let Dario run with Louis when it was no secret the two did not get along.

"Yeah. Louis is my vocal coach after all and my piano teacher. It's not like I don't see him a lot already." Dario shrugged. His statement was all the answer the others needed.

"Remember that first time you sang at school," Gavin asked. Four years was so long ago after all.

"I'm surprised you two do. You never pay attention to anything when you're stuck in a large crowd."

"Oh come on Dario. We were naked in the tub down the hall together. And it's not that often someone has two singers and a musician as a best friend."

"You can play the drums," Dario countered. Gavin shrugged. He was always downplaying his drum skills to beef up Dario's awesomeness. Rayland did the same by pretending she wasn't a better singer than him. Or at least Dario thought he wasn't as good as her. She never let her guard down, though. He was the best, and there was no changing her mind.

"It's hilarious looking at the vid now, but then, at that age, I was on my seat with Rayland screaming you could do it."

"That I will never forget. Do you two always have to be so loud?"

Rayland and Gavin screamed the loudest they could.

"Shut the fuck up in there!" Gavin's mom said and banged on the door. The three of them laughed. Dario hit Gavin with a pillow which did not get the desired effect of stopping him from laughing.

"Louis saved your life. And man can he play the guitar," Rayland commented.

"Yeah. It's so different when I'm with him. He knows more about me than my parents do."

There was a truth hanging on that comment that no one wanted to tackle. An awkward silence lingered because of this.

When they were younger, neither Gavin nor Rayland knew why Dario's mood would switch up sometimes. Depression wasn't something they thought about. That and Dario's anxiety was much more apparent. But now, months before they'd all be ten, depression was a thing they recognised on a fundamental level. Dario wasn't happy, and it was their job to ensure he was when with them. Rayland was the one to break the silence.

"I won't be going to middle school with you guys."

Music Happens When You Remember to Breathe

"Breathe Dario."

Dario was at a lesson on the verge of an anxiety attack. Louis was attempting to calm him down.

"You okay, Dario?"

"I'm fine."

"Is that why you're singing so bad today?"

Dario's panic increased. If he couldn't sing, his life was over. It was the only thing his mom seemed to care about. Being the overachiever he was, Dario's mom had no shortage of things to gloat about. Still, in his mind, the Christian music career was number one. He couldn't fail at this.

"Anxious about starting a new school?" Louis probed to which Dario nodded.

"And the fact Rayland is not going with you?"

Dario gave more nods. It wasn't like she hadn't warned him two years ago she was gearing towards earning a scholarship to a private art school. She said it like she had already earned that scholarship that she hadn't even applied for. Sometimes Dario wished he had that type of confidence.

"And—" Louis said, encouraging Dario to speak.

"What if middle school is too hard? And I start failing classes, and I don't fit in? What if I don't make the football team? I've never been without Ray. Can I even be a friend to someone I don't see every day? There will be shitloads of new people—"

"You're swearing now?" Louis raised an eyebrow and almost smirked.

"Don't tell my mom."

"Your secret is safe with me."

Louis made a show of locking his heart and swallowing the key. This made Dario smile and slowly start to calm down.

"Is that all?"

"I don't want to mess up. My mom doesn't like it when I

get nervous, but I can't help it. Sometimes I wish I had different parents." Dario looked down, immediately depressed.

Louis was much more of a father to Dario than his own. At the moment, this was closer to the truth than he dared express.

Dario couldn't see this desire to be perfect was unhealthy. That hating his parents when his entire existence revolved around garnering their approval was self-destructive. He couldn't see, while looking down at the ground in shame, how much of this affected Louis. If he had looked up, Louis might've reached out and hugged him, but it wasn't meant to be.

"They want my brother to play the violin." Dario almost choked it out. As if it was the worst thing they could ever want for him. He looked back up to Louis as he said it.

"And this is bad?" Louis responded, amused. Dario didn't notice the variance in Louis' tone.

"If they treat him the way they treat me, maybe. It could be different with him. Not sure really. Do you think I talk weird?"

"How you mean?"

"The kids at school make fun of the way I talk. They keep saying I talk like a white boy." Dario took note of the unamused face Louis made at that statement. He wasn't sure what to make of it.

"And that bothers you?"

"I'm okay with how I talk. Doesn't change how their words make me feel. What's the point of doing everything so well if everyone is still going to be mean to me?"

"Let's try the song again, and this time remember to breathe."

Dario nodded as Louis turned and began to play the piano. This time, Dario was perfect. As if his inner songbird had erupted from its nest and took flight.

"A lot of students have come through my door over the years. You are definitely one of my favourites. And one of my first at that. Fresh out of college I was when I started with you."

Every time Louis complimented him, Dario smiled shyly with a twinge of awkwardness. Dario took a moment to really look at Louis. Louis was average height, average build, had skin as brown as healthy earth, and there was something about him that made Dario feel better in his presence.

After a moment Dario realised he was staring much too hard at Louis and he didn't want his thoughts to travel any further than they were. And Louis was looking at him. Smiling. Why was he smiling? Did he know what Dario was trying not to think about?

"I'm sure you train lots of better vocalists than me."

Louis didn't take him up on that seeing as Dario was in a much better space than before the song. It didn't last long. Dario started to get anxious but not as bad as the full out panic attack he was on the verge of earlier.

"Could you teach him the guitar? He saw you play once and he won't stop talking about it to me. He mentioned it to my parents, but it went nowhere. You teach violin too, don't you? Couldn't you just teach him on the side? My parents wouldn't have to know. I'm sure convincing them to let you teach him the Violin wouldn't be too hard. You are already my vocal coach after all."

The fact that Louis would be teaching the guitar on the sly for free seemed to completely slip Dario's mind.

After a brief moment of contemplation Louis said he'd talk to Dario's parents. Dario let out a long breath. He didn't realise how tense and scared he was waiting for the response. Louis motioned for him to come to the piano and grabbed his guitar as Dario sat down to play.

Dario was a lot better now than he was that recital day six years ago. Writing his own songs; most of which were depressing. Sometimes if he were bold enough, he'd play them here. He'd sing them as well on a good day.

Louis never judged him or made him feel weird. He was the only adult who really knew and understood him. Dario told him everything, including things he was afraid to say normally.

Louis came to every game. Never skipped church when he knew Dario was singing. His actions creating a mostly unspoken but obviously seen bond between them.

Their lesson time was over. However, Dario was the last student allowing him time to stay awhile longer. Dario didn't know that Louis did this intentionally. He allowed time for anxiety, panic attacks and space in case Dario needed to receive things he didn't get at home. The side effect of Dario being there so much was that Louis' children, at least inside the house, acted like Dario was family. Them being so close in age for a time the boys genuinely thought he was their brother who just lived somewhere else. The two oldest were devastated to find out there was no blood relation. For about thirty seconds before reclaiming Dario as family.

As Dario sat down to play, for the first time he fully accepted why his dad didn't like Louis. He almost started to panic at the thought, but the sound of Louis playing a random riff to warm up his fingers stalled it.

Dario started to play an original and listen to Louis improvise and chose, for the moment, to forget about anxiety, panic, depression, sadness; to let go of the boy he pretended to be and breathe.

I Want To Be A Normal Boy

Dario was hiding in his room, having an anxiety attack. The first day of school was always overwhelming, but this time it was a new school. How could he not panic?

He needed therapy, but both his mother and father frowned upon that. Apparently, all he needed was God and to stop being weak; and, most importantly, prayer.

Dario was also afraid of what he might say if he saw a therapist. He was constructing a fantasy family image with him as the perfect son, student, athlete, and older brother. The good Christian boy out to fulfil his parents dream of Christian music superstardom. Yet here he was, sitting on the edge of his bed having a panic attack. Hyperventilating and wondering why he was so unhappy when he had nothing to be unhappy about. That was what he was terrified of, the truth.

Dario didn't want someone probing in his head fucking things up with real facts. His fake truths were enough. His mom came and banged on the door, bringing Dario out of his thoughts. He had long been ready as he made a habit of always being earlier than need be in case he found himself unable to move.

His mother was shouting something to him about sucking it up and dealing with it. There was more mumble about going out to prayer-night because she was positive it was evil spirits causing his issues. Dario zoned out when she got to that part.

Dario eventually got up and headed over to the mirror in his room. He finally, at age eleven, had the one thing he always wanted. Contacts. He looked into the mirror at his perfectly brown eyes. He had been wearing them religiously for a whole week.

Dario hated looking at his own eyes.

With the combination of his mother making it clear he didn't deserve them and the children teasing him, there wasn't anything anyone could say to make him feel good about them. Dario had thought something in him would change. That he'd feel more whole with brown eyes. So far, his existence hadn't magically become better. Maybe it would take some time. He knew one thing though, no one would be teasing him about his blue eyes ever again.

System Check: Human Drone Program… No Errors Found

Dario and his family were out to dinner celebrating his mother's new book deal. The project was still in research phase, but her pitch was enough to get signed. She made her money as a motivational Christian speaker. She had always made reasonably decent money, but her manager just landed her, her first high paying headlining job at a major Christian convention.

Dario was, as always, immaculately pressed and dressed for an upscale dinner. His mom was sparing no expense on this celebration and had been gloating to anyone who would listen, the entire week. Modesty was not one of her strong points.

Considering how semi lucrative her career was they lived way below their means. In a house almost too small for five. Dario was okay with this. He had no idea what living with money was like, so had nothing to compare it to.

Things were going well. His parents were celebrating with champagne. Dario decided on meat and veg for dinner and a fruit platter for dessert, no starter. That fit his week's calculations. He loved math, so counting the nutritional value of his meals was fun.

Dario was busy taking the first slice of his steak when he heard his mother make a sound that he knew too well. Something unpleasant must've happened. Dario's first thought was had he forgotten to pray before eating, but he knew he had so it must've been an outside force. Even his little brother was past the stage of doing things that would bother them. Dario's sister was only one, so it couldn't be her causing the problem.

As he scoped the restaurant, he found the culprit of his mother's ire. A lesbian and gay couple sharing a table together. Dario knew where how the night's conversation would go. As the conversation turned towards homosexuality being an abomination, Dario did his best to ignore them. Unfortunately, his parents were speaking so loud a waiter had to ask them to be quiet. Other patrons were complaining about them.

As Dario's parents carried on, he subconsciously joined them. Almost everything he was, was wrapped in how they made him; how he made himself to be for them. Always he listened with attention. Spoke in agreement when necessary, and made sure to engrave all their opinions so deep on his soul they burned and left scars which he was unaware of. Scars that would never fully heal. This night was no different.

His parents used the same material and akin to his own sense of order, had them stacked together for the most optimal effect. Because of this, Dario knew when to speak and how much emphasis was needed at the specific moments with zero effort. It got so bad his parents refused to eat there while *those* people were there. The manager wasn't having any of that negative energy in their establishment though.

The two couples, however, remained calm. Which, did nothing to stop Dario's parents from ranting as they made their very epic inglorious exit. Refusing to finish eating and saying they would never patronise the restaurant again as they left in a huff. Dario dutifully gave evil glares to the couples when he walked by and added a few additions to his parents' statements on cue. They were a well-oiled and perfected hate machine. His brother was still learning what to do, so he kept quiet or took his cues from Dario.

Once all where in the car, Dario's mother talked about how this would be good material for her next book. Another self-published short while she was working on the big secret project. Dario told her it was a good idea and reaffirmed his dislike for homosexuals. She nodded her head in approval, as did his father. They were always flowing with praise and the love Dario craved when he aligned with their extremes. This love was addictive. His yearning to have more was at a very toxic level.

Nothing more was said during the drive home. There really

wasn't much left after everything said already. Even if there was, Dario had already put on his headset and started listening to music. Singing to himself. His parents didn't complain about the noise because they were in such a great mood after what they felt was a good deed done. God's work had been done. Dario was thankful for a moment to sing in peace.

Once home, Dario went straight to his room and readied himself for bed. As he tried to sleep the only thought on his mind was homosexuality is evil. For Dario to continue building his perfect image, he could not be gay. The thought not on his mind, however, was that the next day he'd be thirteen.

Samuel Alexander

26

Showtunes, Unplanned Visits, Truths, and Hugs

Dario was standing looking at a piece of sheet music. Just another musical number Rayland said he should add to her ever-growing song-list for him. Dario tried to protest because he was going to be a gospel singer, but Rayland was very hard to argue with. She was convinced she could get him to join team Drama. Even with anxiety issues once he got going, Dario was amazing. He could be the next Broadway star, but that was not the path his parents had set out for him.

Louis wasn't prepared for him to stop by. He was in the back-yard drinking hard lemonade with his girl and their children. A perfectly relaxing afternoon. It was spring break and they were having a staycation with their children. Neither had expected Dario to show up knocking on the door, intent on coming in for this impromptu lesson. Dario's mind was acutely focused on the fact he needed someone to talk to. Someone who took him as is without all the pressure. His own father was just his mom's sidekick.

Dario's parents tried to change vocal coaches a few months past, but his anxiety blocked him from learning with another teacher. Dario had also gotten used to their Saturday morning runs. The attempted breakaway was too much, and neither of his parents could argue with the fact most of Louis' students were remarkable.

This day, however, Dario just needed to sing. His parents were taking their anti-gay activism more seriously lately. It had been just over a year since the restaurant incident, and he was tired of joining their campaigns so he faked a holiday lesson and Rayland supplied the difficult sheet music to corroborate his story. Now he was with Louis. Offloading his emotions and interspersing with song. Rayland was right. The song was perfect for him.

"But how do you feel?" Louis asked during one of their breaks.

"If that's what my parents believe that's what I believe," Dario responded. It was his standard response to anything that took him outside of his comfort zone. Louis, Dario noticed, didn't look like he would let up this time.

Dario wasn't a fan of lying. If probed enough either his anxiety would take over and force people to stop prying, or he'd get angry and refuse to answer. But, on the rare occasion, Dario would reveal a truth he'd ordinarily hide. It was a lot less rare around Louis.

"But your opinion matters. You just went fourteen. You're about to graduate from middle school. Surely you're capable of making some decisions on your own—"

"I make decisions all the time." It was a true enough response, but Louis was not so stupid to miss the obvious.

"But are they your own?"

"Yes, no..."

Dario took a few moments of silence. The conclusion he came to wasn't one he was fond of. He decided he would hold onto it.

"I don't know."

Dario hadn't meant to say it but the realisation that he was unsure of what his own voice was, was unsettling. Louis didn't offer a response. He started to play the piano and let him sing a bit more.

"You're definitely getting better. Are you sure you don't want to get into acting? Broadway could be good for you."

"You sound like Ray. She's the only reason I'm in dance classes."

"Good on her," Louis said as Latoya came and dropped off some more of her home made hard lemonade; making a show of telling Dario how cute he was and how tall he was getting. Dario smiled awkwardly.

"So how do you feel about people being gay?" Louis asked again after she left. Dario seemed like he might be willing to answer this time. And their lesson time was almost up.

"I don't care. People are people. But with every passing grade. Every dance class, every higher belt in self-defence, each time I score a touchdown, the more Bible I know, the cleaner I am, and most importantly the more Christian I am, my parents shower me with praise. It makes them happy. I have the perfect situation. Why mess with a good thing?"

Dario knew his friends and Louis could see the truth about his unhappiness. But if he gave in to that emotion what would happen to this persona he had built? Dario didn't like the look Louis was giving him but was saved from looking at it too long because his mom arrived. He'd see Louis again for their Saturday morning runs. His weekly dose of Louis beyond lessons.

He hated leaving Louis. Hated going back to the perfect home that made him feel so imperfect. Yet the thought of it all falling apart was too unbearable to risk changing it.

Before Dario headed for the door, he gave Louis a hug. Dario didn't initiate hugs because he was weird about touching people, but he needed this hug.

They were almost the same height. Dario would soon be taller than him, but for now, when they released each other, it was easy for Louis to look into Dario's eyes.

They were brown.

When Alone Becomes More Than Alone

Dario's first day of high school was a disaster. It started with one of the worst panic attacks he'd ever had followed by his mother dragging him outside to the car. Somehow Dario's mother had forgotten to renew his contacts prescription. Something she had never done during three years of middle school. The visions of blue-eyed torment had Dario hyperventilating the entire drive to school.

After being dropped off Dario made his way to homeroom, avoiding all eye contact. His only focus was getting his breathing under control. In homeroom, he picked a chair the furthest away from other students. He could see them looking at him. Feel their judgment on his appearance, his eyes, his everything. Almost as if they knew the secrets he had. He pushed his glasses back from the brim of his nose and tried to focus on the music he was listening too, hoping it would make the entire day just swim by smoothly.

Trouble first began during lunch period. A group of kids were laughing, making jokes about Dario's prepared lunch. Throwing a few insults amongst themselves but loud enough for Dario to hear. Teasing was something Dario was used to. He was hoping he'd be able to avoid it escalating until one boy in the group said Dario was probably gay.

Dario instinctively got up, headed towards the group and punched him in the face. To anyone else, it looked like Dario started the fight unprovoked. No one was paying that much attention to this small clique of freshmen. It wasn't long before there was a crowd. Dario made quick work of the beat down and walked away before an adult showed up. He didn't want to get caught in a fight on the first day. The guy who got his ass kicked didn't look like he was about to run and tell so chances were Dario wouldn't get in trouble.

On his way to his next class, another incident happened. A male student looked at him in a way Dario did not appreciate. He shouted at him the same rehearsed stuff his parents had bred into him about homosexuality. He regretted it immediately, but the student was gone before Dario could take it back.

Dario was pretty out of it for the rest of the day. Too much adrenaline to focus on anything. He spent the end of this first day turning into a shaky useless mess when he got teased. This was probably better than the opposite fight reaction, though it didn't feel that way.

When Dario thought he'd escaped any chance of more drama, a group of students started making fun of his eyes, and the opposite did happen. Dario ran up and hit one of them, but this time they banded together and he couldn't fight them all off. By the time a teacher came to break it up, Dario was severely beaten. Nothing broken but more than enough bruises. It looked like his attackers were about to be punished, but Dario wasn't concerned with that. He just wanted the day to be over.

His mother asked what had happened when Dario got in the car. Dario had cleaned up a bit, but it was obvious he had recently been in a fight. Her only response was that the other child was probably gay himself and deserved the beat down. It was clear anyone who questioned Dario's sexuality deserved a good punch in the face in her eyes. As far as the blue-eyed hate, she said what she always said, "White people have blue eyes." Then got out of the car without looking back to see if her child was following. Dario was half white, because of her but clearly not white enough for blue eyes.

After going through his class schedule, a map of the school so he would never get lost, and coming up with a rough draft of his studying schedule, Dario finally ate and got to bed. As soon as he hit the pillows, he cried. The whole day was overwhelming and neither his mom nor dad was helpful. He picked up his phone, but instead of calling his friends, he called Louis. He had to get something off his chest. The reason why he was so upset.

The last fight, when being teased about his eyes like so many times before, Gavin had been there. He stood by, watched, and did nothing. Dario's parents were one thing but his best friend? That hurt him to the core. It was the most painful thing he'd experienced in life, and Dario saw no way of getting over it. The feeling of being betrayed.

When A Good Hit Realigns Broken Shit

Things didn't get much better for Dario despite his best efforts. He'd managed to get on the football team and made some 'almost' friends. There was a large sect of school kids that thought he was the sexiest thing ever. This was lost on Dario because he saw himself as anything but.

He talked to almost no one. Sat with the jocks who only spoke to themselves. Didn't hang with anyone outside of school because church consumed his time. Students made fun of him just because they could and they had a wealth of things to choose from. After all, what jock sits and reads a book and listens to music while his friends are at the same table talking sports? Who reads passages of the bible on every break and has no social life outside of the church? Why did he not have a high school girlfriend yet when everyone seemed to think he was one of the hottest in the year? Why was he so neat?

Dario never thought that being boring could be cause for teasing but, apparently, in high school everything was up for grabs. He was that odd conundrum of popular and unpopular. The gay school community was hostile towards him because his parents were extremely vocal with their opinions at the first parent-student meeting.

Having apologised to the guy he shouted at in the hall, Dario knew the other students were aware he was not like his parents. Yet they were still out to get him because he was the easier target.

Dario was also dealing with people making fun of his panic attacks. Watching overdramatised versions of how he hyperventilated before tests did nothing to stop them happening. It was in the times when his anxiety rendered him incapable of fighting that the teasing was at its highest. He told his mom once. She acted like it was his fault for not praying hard enough to rid himself of anxiety.

It was almost Thanksgiving and the students were letting up if not quitting entirely. Clearly bored of Dario and moving on to new victims.

Dario was hoping today would be one of the better days. A boring Wednesday. Next thing he knew some random first year was making fun. Shoving Dario, faking like he didn't see him as he walked by. Dario would've hit him, but Gavin did. Punched him hard and looked like he was itching for a reason to do it again.

The troublemaker looked back to his friends who didn't seem to have his back. Gavin was real trouble. Unlike Dario, he didn't need a good reason to kick someone's ass. He was also the resident weed pusher. No one was trying to get on his bad side and have him cut them off. Walking away was the smart thing to do.

Dario was still in a bit of shock. Gavin had ignored him for almost three months now. He'd cried about it more than once. Asked Rayland if she knew what had happened. If there was something he'd done and whatever it was he was sorry. Dario had sent more text messages and voice notes to Gavin than he could count with zero results. He really missed Gavin, and here Gavin was. Hitting a guy for him like things were still the same.

"Friends?"

Gavin put out his hand, offering Dario nothing more than a chance to be friends again. Dario reached out, shook his hand and even though confused as hell, felt instantly better. Gavin left him there to decide where he wanted to sit for lunch. The jocks, or Gavin's crew of delinquents. Dario chose to sit with Gavin.

As he turned to follow him, he saw someone just past Gavin's table sitting down with a white girl and a boy so gay there probably wasn't a word gay enough to describe him. The guy in question though, that boy reminded him of Louis, and that thought alone was enough to make him stay as far away from him as humanly possible. So much so Gavin nudged him when he sat down to eat his food and asked Dario why he was praying so intently. Dario didn't say anything but Gavin... he knew. Yeah... he knew.

Sexy Hands Are Everything

Dario walked into his last class for the week not really feeling it. It was the first week of senior year. He was on time but late by Dario standards. Another teacher held him back with college talk. He was only mildly annoyed, but college talk? The first week in school? Was that even necessary? Couldn't the teacher wait until next semester?

Dario had a rough year. Something was going on at home which forced him to up his perfect image. He had taken it to obsessive levels last term before summer. It wasn't the best idea, but it was the only solution Dario could come up with. The one way to stop the world he knew from falling apart. That's what he had believed but now, after a half-year of efforts, Dario realised it was a lost cause. The immediate problem became what was he going to do with his life now that everything he knew was no more.

This year he'd cried more and been the most depressed he'd ever been. He and Gavin were in friendship limbo. This made worse by the fact when Dario came in contact with him, despite his best efforts not to, Gavin would act like things were cool. As if he knew Dario was struggling and he'd come around eventually. Dario didn't have as much faith in himself.

He was broken from his train of thought when he walked into the class. Dario hated being the last to arrive and was starting to feel anxious. The need to find somewhere to sit was imperative. If he didn't sort that out fast, he'd have to deal with being late and standing looking like a lost puppy. Too much to end the last class of the week with. The only seat left was in one of the back corners. By the one person he'd successfully avoided all of high school. This guy looked up at him and smiled. Dario on reflex smiled back.

"Don't get jealous girls. That smile's only for me," the boy said coyly and gave a macho wink in Dario's direction. Dario winced a bit.

"Don't be shy. I saved this seat just for you. Don't act like you don't want to sit by me hot stuff."

Dario rolled his eyes, making his way to the empty desk.

"Stay away from me, Satan," Dario said as he sat down.

"What? I haven't even brought out my best evil," the boy responded with a mischievous grin. Dario did not laugh and gave a convincing unamused stare.

"Is there any chance you'll leave me alone? Just a little bit?"

"Is there any chance of you not looking like a teen muscle god in that shirt?"

Dario side-eyed him and proceeded to get out his textbooks.

"That's what I thought muscles. Could you be any neater?"

Dario was lining up all his equipment perfectly on the desk.

"Class is about to start, and you have nothing on your desk. Shouldn't you be getting ready?"

"Oh I'm learning all I need looking at you."

Dario chuckled. He was feeling awkward and embarrassed. His only desire was to get on with class. Yet this guy continued with his flirtations. Dario's rebuttals were only getting laughs from the other students. Usually Dario would've defended his straightness, but he was feeling so awful entering class that somehow this was uplifting his spirits. Bringing him away from the funk of the entire year for a moment.

"You have nice hands."

That was the last thing his classmate said before the teacher forced everyone to stop laughing at the two of them. Dario, for the first time in a while, smiled a genuine smile. The best thing about this whole dialogue was that this was his first-class all week which did not garner an anxiety attack.